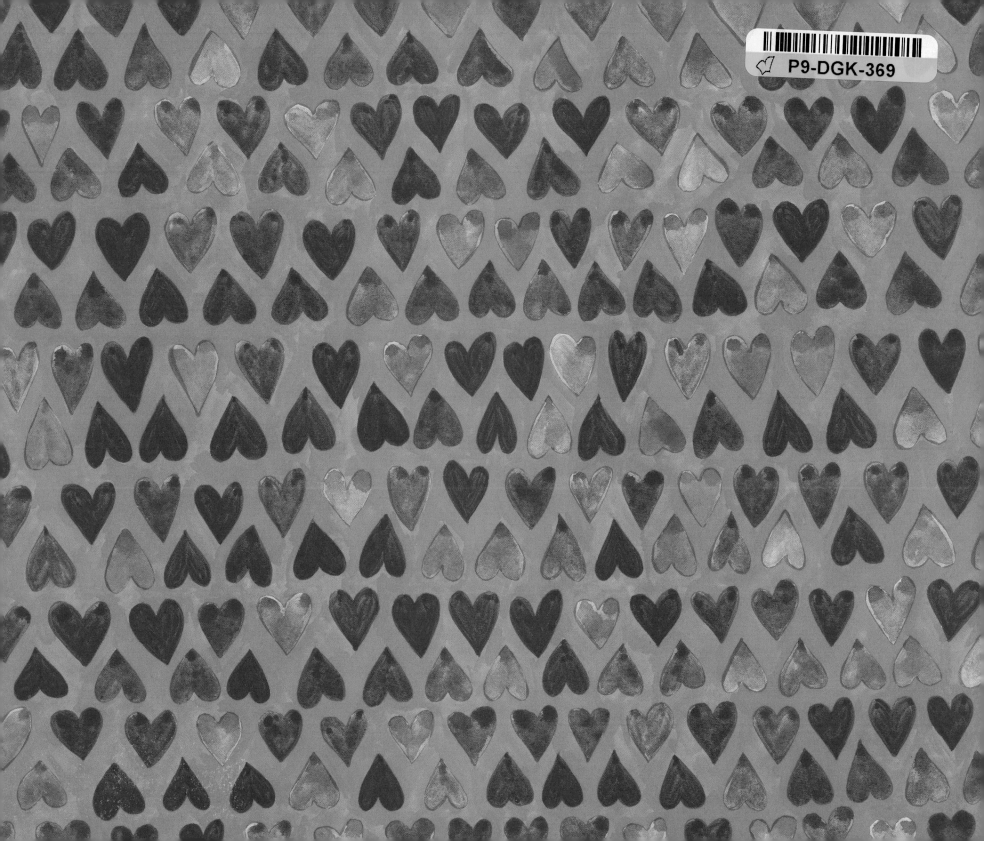

This book is dedicated to the irreplaceable Keeley Schenwar.
You are missed.

Cheryl Klein took valuable time out of her busy schedule to offer substantive edits to this manuscript.
I am profoundly grateful. Thank you also to Nate Marshall and Santera Matthews for their editorial suggestions.
I asked a number of wonderful children to read and offer feedback on this story. I want to thank:
Nora Essen Cloud, Charles Malcolm Cloud, Fiora Curotto, Wyatt Beekman-Dowell, Simone Fizdale,
Savahli Liger, Maya-Ki Millikan, Gus Hunter-Palmer, Kimani Arroyo-Parris, Nia Arroyo-Parris,
Kiran Atlas-Patel, Zola Pineda, Leandro Pineda, Elias Price, Solomon Price, Max Raven, Lily Jacoby-Reese
—**Mariame**

Thank you to my family and my communities.
—**Bianca**

Published in 2022 by Haymarket Books
P.O. Box 180165, Chicago, IL 60618
www.haymarketbooks.org
ISBN: 978-1-64259-763-9
Distributed by Consortium Book Sales and Distribution.
Library of Congress Cataloging-in-Publication data is available.

Printed in Canada.

10 9 8 7 6 5 4 3 2 1

SEE YOU SOON

WRITTEN BY MARIAME KABA

ILLUSTRATED BY BIANCA DIAZ

HAYMARKET BOOKS
CHICAGO, ILLINOIS

Queenie is what they call me,
But Reyna is my name.
I am six years old.
And my life's about to change.

My Mama, she's been sick since I was very small.

Sometimes she goes away when she isn't feeling well at all.

A girl at school named Keisha sometimes says mean things to me.

"Your Mama, she takes drugs! Your Mama is a junkie!"

Keisha's words sting my heart,
And leave me feeling sad.
"Don't pay her any mind," says Grandma Louise.
"Your Mama, she's sick, and that doesn't mean she's bad."

When Mama isn't sick,
We are two peas in a pod.
We shop at the grocery store,
Roam aisles, even and odd.

We share ice cream sundaes,
And play games at the park.
We wash clothes at the laundromat,
And watch the fireflies in the dark.

Today we're riding on a train,
Grandma, Mama, and me.
We'll board the bus to the county jail,
Once we get out of the city.

Grandma is reading the Bible.
Mama's looking out the window.
No one is speaking, not one word.
We don't have much farther to go.

I have so many questions.
I'd ask, but I'm afraid.
I push my fingers through my Mama's,
Weaving them tight like a braid.

Standing tall in front of the jail,
I breathe in and find the strength.
I ask Mama, "Where will you sleep?"
She looks like her heart will break.

"Can I see your room?" I ask.
Mama's eyes are bright with tears.
"No, baby girl, no one is allowed..."
She speaks, but I don't hear.

I wonder what Mama's cell looks like.
Will it be cold inside?
Are there warm blankets for her?
My heart is pounding. I want to run and hide.

I look into Mama's eyes.
I don't want to see her cry.
I don't want Mama to go to jail.
She should always be by my side.

Who will help me braid my hair?
Who will I ask about homework?
Mama makes it fun to learn.
My chest begins to hurt.

Mama opens her arms and wraps me up.
She hugs me so, so tight.
"You be good. Take care of Grandma.
Baby girl, I'll be all right."

So many questions are swirling in my head.
I have time for just one more.
"When will I see you again, Mama?"
"Soon, Queenie. Soon," she says to me.
"Time will fly. Don't you worry, my Queenie."
Grandma Louise takes my hand, and we walk to the door.

"Two years is not soon!" I yell, so mad my face turns red.
Grandma gives me a look,
And I say "sorry" and hang my head.

I don't want to leave my Mama.
She'll be in there all alone.
But Grandma says that it's time to go.
We've got to catch the bus and train home.

Mama kisses my cheeks wet with tears.
She turns and walks through the gate.
I want to beg her not to go, to stay with us.
Grandma and I are quiet as we ride home.
When we arrive, I run into my room,
Just wanting to be alone.

But there's a brand-new quilt on my bed.
It has photos of Mama and me!
Opening presents at Christmas, eating birthday cake,
Mama holding me when I was a baby.

I throw myself on the bed,
And wrap myself in memories.
I fall asleep dreaming of my Mama.
Her voice saying, "Sweet dreams, Queenie."

The next day at school, my mind is wandering.
The teacher calls on me, but I don't hear.
Is Mama lonely without me? Is she doing okay?
My heart is heavy with worry and fear.

Two long weeks go by,
and then one day when school is done,
I find a letter on my bed.
It's my Mama's handwriting, shining bright like the sun.

Queenie

The letter reads: To my baby girl, Queenie... From Mama.

I open it slowly, gently.

I sit down on my bed to read it,

And my heart fills with peace.

Dear baby girl,
This is your mama and I love you.
I loved you before I even met you.
I love you still
And I always will.
Even though I'm away,
my love is always here to stay.
See you soon, Queenie.
Love,
Mama
me
you
Grandma
Louise
eating raspas at the
park ♡
RASPADOS♡

Grandma comes into my room.

She has a grilled cheese sandwich for me to eat.

She says, "Do you want to visit your Mama next Saturday?"

I jump up and down, and shout, "YES! YES! YES!"

I rain down kisses all over Grandma's face.

When bedtime comes,

I hold the letter as darkness fills my room.

I fall asleep hearing my Mama's voice,

"See you soon, Queenie, see you soon."

Ways to Help

1. Start a fundraising campaign to support organizations that work with children who have incarcerated loved ones. Some ideas include: You and a friend can run a lemonade stand to raise money, or put together a talent show with other kids to sell tickets to raise money, or ask your parents and their friends to donate some funds. You can also donate funds to these organizations:

   Amachi Mentoring Program
   http://www.amachimentoring.org/locations.html

   Project Avary
   https://www.projectavary.org

   Aunt Mary's Storybook
   https://cjtinc.org/projects/amsb/

   Free Minds Book Club and Writing Workshop
   https://freemindsbookclub.org/about-us/

   Hour Children
   https://hourchildren.org

   Seedling
   https://seedlingmentors.org/give/

2. Donate books to incarcerated children:

   Liberation Library
   https://www.liberationlib.com

3. Donate a copy of this book to your local library so that other children can read it too.

4. Donate toys to children with incarcerated loved ones during the holidays.

Mariame Kaba

Mariame Kaba is an educator and organizer based in New York City. She has been active in the anti-criminalization and anti-violence movements for over 30 years. Mariame is the founder and director of Project NIA, a grassroots organization with a long-term vision to end youth incarceration. She is the author of *Missing Daddy* (Haymarket, 2019) and *We Do This 'Til We Free Us* (Haymarket, 2021).

Learn more at www.mariamekaba.com.

Bianca Diaz

Bianca Diaz is a Mexican American artist from Chicago's Pilsen neighborhood. She is the illustrator of the children's books *Starting Over in Sunset Park* (Tilbury, 2021) and *The One Day House* (Charlesbridge, 2017). She lives in Brooklyn, New York.

See more at biancadiaz.com.